DEFENDERS OF THE GALAXY

The galaxy has many heroes — be they powerful, Force-wielding Jedi Knights, or bold and valiant rebels. But let it never be forgotten that there would be no heroes without their brave assistants!

CABLE CONNECTIONS

OOPS! I MUST'VE DROPPED THE SCREWDRIVER SOMEWHERE ON THE WIRES . . .

There are three astromech droids struggling to fix this Jedi starship. Help them repair it by drawing lines to fix the wires, making sure the symbols at the end of each wire match.

OH, BROTHER, NOT AGAIN! I HOPE ARTOO CAN FIX THEM.

A MIRAGE

After a long, tiresome journey through the hot desert, the group found Yoda selling lemonade. But was it all just a mirage? Look at the small pictures melting in the hot air and mark where they can be found in the big picture.

1

2

3

4

STRONG WITH THE FORCE

THE GREAT RACE

Help Anakin Skywalker win the speeder race by finding the shortest way to the finish line. Be quick, the young pilot is revving his engine!

AREN'T YOU A BIT TOO OLD TO PLAY GAMES IN THE SAND, MASTER QUI-GON?

IT'S NOT A GAME! IT'S A DETAILED MOCK-UP OF A TRACK!

FINISH

START

FIRST FLIGHT

Anakin launched the starship by guessing the passcode. Look at the sequences in the table and finish each row to figure out the code.

ON THE RADAR

Anakin's astromech droid, R2-D2, operates the radar. Help the droid recognize the shadows on the screen by drawing lines to connect them with the matching ships.

KNIGHT-IN-TRAINING

When he was younger, Anakin studied at the Jedi Academy. On his first day, he took all his books to his class because he didn't know which one he would need. C-3PO took this funny picture . . .

At first glance this photo looks identical to the one on the left.
But an expert eye will see 11 differences between them.
Find and mark them all.

DESERT SEARCH

Anakin Skywalker has lost his trusty droid in the sand dunes! He put a special chip in R2-D2's systems, so he should be able to find him. Look at the map, find the droid's location, and write its coordinates in the empty box.

A NEW MODEL

Anakin lost his lightsaber in a duel with Count Dooku. Design a new weapon for the young Jedi Knight, so he can fight the evil Count again. Make it look awesome!

YOU BREAK IT – YOU PAY FOR IT!

FREE SEATS

There are still spaces left on board the transporter. Draw in the missing clone troopers, making sure the number of clones in each row and column matches the number at the end of the row and column they are in. The empty boxes are the free seats!

MASTER VERSUS STUDENT

After joining the dark side, Anakin — now known as Darth Vader — attacked his teacher. It seems not everyone should be allowed to swing a lightsaber around! Draw lines to show where each cut-off piece should be.

LOOK! YOU'VE RUINED THE WHOLE PICTURE!

AN UNUSUAL MISSION

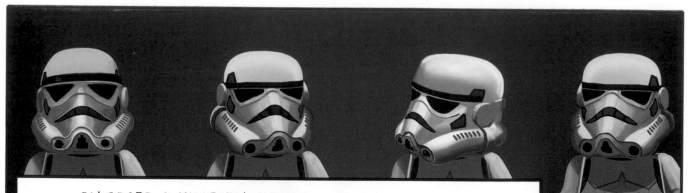

ON BOARD A MILITARY CARRIER, A TEAM OF FEARLESS STORMTROOPERS ARE BEING TRANSPORTED TO A SECRET DESTINATION. WHAT WILL THEIR MISSION BE THIS TIME?

WE'RE LANDING IN 30 SECONDS. GET READY!

I'VE GOT A BAD FEELING ABOUT THIS . . .

YOU SHOULD BE EXCITED. TRUST ME, YOU'RE GONNA LIKE IT.

YEAH! IT'S TIME FOR SOME REAL ACTION.

DISTORTED HOLOGRAM

R2-D2 found Obi-Wan Kenobi, so he can pass along the encrypted message from Leia Organa. Remove the distortions in the message by numbering the hologram pieces to put them in the right order.

FIX IT AS QUICKLY AS YOU CAN! IT COULD BE SOME GOOD NEWS ABOUT MY FAVORITE COOKIES!

STAR DRILL

The training drill on the Death Star didn't go very well. Look at the battle formations, then starting from the second row down, circle the new trooper that has joined each row.

IF YOU STAND NICELY, THE LEMONADE'S ON ME!

LIGHTSABER SEARCH

Luke hid his lightsaber in a swamp and left R2-D2 with a note to help him find it. Answer the true or false questions to find the hiding place. When the answer is "FALSE" follow a red arrow, and when it is "TRUE" follow a blue arrow.

LUKE SKYWALKER DOESN'T LIKE R2-D2.

ANAKIN SKYWALKER TURNED TO THE DARK SIDE OF THE FORCE.

R2-D2 BROUGHT OBI-WAN KENOBI A SECRET MESSAGE FROM LEIA ORGANA.

YODA IS A WISE BLUE-SKINNED JEDI MASTER.

JEDI KNIGHTS FIGHT WITH LIGHTSABERS.

FULL THROTTLE

Chased by a group of TIE fighters, Han Solo flew the *Millennium Falcon* into an asteroid maze, and now he needs your help to get him out! The *Falcon* can only fly over the asteroids with craters to get from the start to the finish safely. Draw the route through by connecting all the safe asteroids.

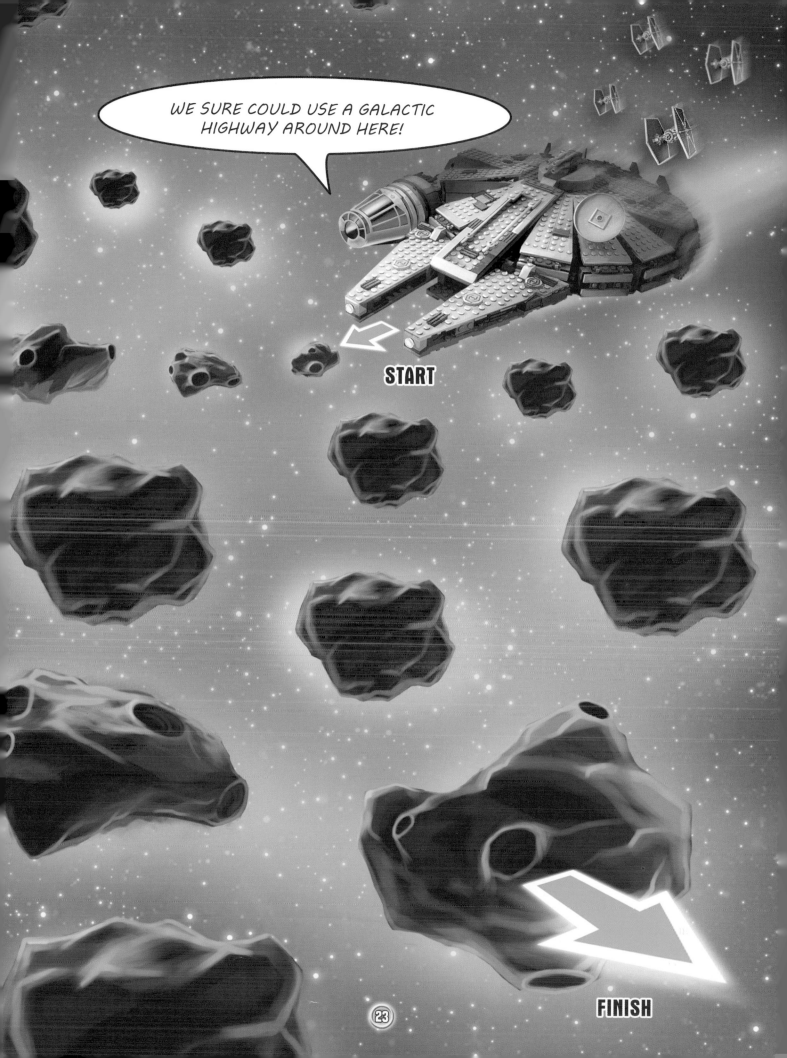

DRESS REHEARSAL

Darth Vader wants to convince his son, Luke Skywalker, to join the dark side. He's practicing his speech in front of the mirror. Which two reflections of Vader are identical? (There's also a picture with a different item on the mirror shelf. Can you tell which one?)

JEDI TRAINING

Luke Skywalker must use the Force to clear the tree trunks off the forest path. Luke can't move a trunk that's lying under another trunk — he must lift the top trunk first. Number the logs in the order the Jedi needs to move them.

FORCE CONSTELLATIONS

The Force is strong in the galaxy. It's even powerful enough to create constellations of great Jedi heroes. Look at the stars and find the constellation that is different from all the others. Which two constellations are identical?

WAIT, ARTOO! IS THAT YODA? I GOTTA TAKE A PICTURE!

STAR QUIZ

1. Choose the right name of this Jedi Master:
   a) Qui-Gon Jim
   b) Qui-Gon Jinn
   c) Quin-Gon Jin

2. What kind of droid is R2-D2?
   a) protocol droid
   b) medical droid
   c) astromech droid

3. What starships are used to move troopers across the galaxy?
   a) transporters
   b) starfighters
   c) tankers

4. Who was Anakin Skywalker's Jedi Master?
   a) Yoda
   b) Mace Windu
   c) Obi-Wan Kenobi

5. A hologram is used to:
   a) detect the influence of the dark side
   b) pass along information
   c) cool rooms

6. Who was the *Millennium Falcon's* pilot?
   a) Han Solo
   b) Chewbacca
   c) Luke Skywalker

7. What name did Anakin Skywalker take after turning to the dark side ofthe Force?
   a) Luke
   b) Vader
   c) Sidious

ANSWERS

p. 2 CABLE CONNECTIONS

p. 12 DESERT SEARCH

E-2

pgs. 20-21 LIGHTSABER SEARCH

p. 4 A MIRAGE

p. 14 FREE SEATS

pgs. 22-23 FULL THROTTLE

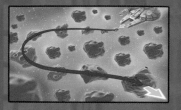

pgs. 6-7 THE GREAT RACE

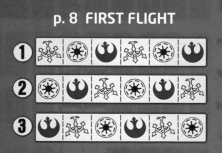

p. 15 MASTER VERSUS STUDENT

p. 24 DRESS REHEARSAL

p. 8 FIRST FLIGHT

p. 18 DISTORTED HOLOGRAM

p. 25 JEDI TRAINING

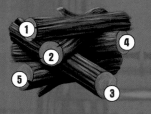

p. 9 ON THE RADAR

p. 19 STAR DRILL

pgs. 26-27 FORCE CONSTELLATIONS

pgs. 10-11 KNIGHT-IN-TRAINING

pgs. 28-29 STAR QUIZ
1 – b, 2 – c, 3 – a, 4 – c, 5 – b, 6 – a, 7 – b.

HOW TO BUILD R2-D2